Someday We'll Have Very Good Manners

by Harriet Ziefert • illustrated by Chris Demarest

G. P. Putnam's Sons • New York

For my well-mannered grandsons,
Will and Nate
—H. Z.

For Rebecca and Elliot
—C. D.

Text copyright © 2001 by Harriet Ziefert
Illustrations copyright © 2001 by Chris Demarest
All rights reserved. This book, or parts thereof, may not be reproduced
in any form without permission in writing from the publisher,
G. P. Putnam's Sons, a division of Penguin Putnam Books for Young Readers,
345 Hudson Street, New York, NY 10014. G. P. Putnam's Sons, Reg. U.S. Pat. & Tm. Off.
Published simultaneously in Canada. Printed in China for Harriet Ziefert, Inc.
The art was done in watercolors.
Library of Congress Cataloging-in-Publication Data
available upon request.
L. C. Number 00-041520
ISBN 0-399-23558-2
1 3 5 7 9 10 8 6 4 2
First Impression

When we grow up, we're going to have very good manners.

I'll be so polite.

I'll always say "please."

And "thank you."

When I answer the telephone, I'll say:
"Hello. Who's calling please?"

And if I make a call, I'll say:
"Hello. May I please speak to Emily?"

We'll remember to wipe our feet.

We won't barge in.
We'll remember to knock.

I'll wait patiently in line.

I won't lose my temper.

I'll take turns.

I'll offer my seat.

I'll hold the door open.

When we grow up, we're going to have very good table manners.

I'll put a napkin in my lap.
And I'll use it!

I'll cut with my knife and eat with my fork.

I'll try liver.

I'll say "please."

I'll say "excuse me."

I'll wait until everyone is served.

And I won't run off before everyone is finished.

When we grow up, our parents will be proud of our good manners.

When we grow up, we won't scream. Or yell. Or shout.

We won't interrupt.

When we get presents, we'll remember to say "thank you for thinking of me."

If we don't like a present, we won't say anything
mean out loud.

Someday we'll be grown-up.

Someday we'll have manners.

But for now, we're just kids!